Zoe's Webs

First published in 1990

Ashton Scholastic Limited
Private Bag 1, Penrose, Auckland 5, New Zealand.

Ashton Scholastic Pty Ltd
PO Box 579, Gosford, NSW 2250, Australia.

Scholastic Inc.
730 Broadway, New York, NY 10003, USA

Scholastic-TAB Publications Ltd
123 Newkirk Road, Richmond Hill, Ontario L4C 3G5, Canada.

Scholastic Publications Ltd
Marlborough House, Holly Walk, Leamington Spa, Warwickshire CV32 4LS, England.

Text copyright © Thomas West, 1989
Illustration copyright © Judy Lambert, 1989

National Library of New Zealand
Cataloguing-in-Publication data

West, Thomas.
   Zoe's webs / by Thomas West ; illustrated by Judy Lambert. Auckland, N.Z. :
Ashton Scholastic, 1990.
   i v. (Read by reading)
   Picture story book for children.
   ISBN 1-86943-013-1
   1. Readers (Elementary) I. Lambert, Judy. II Title. III Series:
Read by reading series
   428.6 (NZ823.2)

54321   01234/9

Typeset in Century Old Style by Rennies Illustrations Ltd
Printed in Hong Kong

Zoe's Webs

by Thomas West
Illustrated by Judy Lambert

READ BY READING
Ashton Scholastic
Auckland   Sydney   New York   London   Toronto

In a big, silky tent
lived the spider family and Zoe.

The silky tent was a happy home
until the night a strong wind blew most of it away.
The spider family and Zoe were all blown out.

Zoe landed alone on a flowering plant.

4

Zoe had never learned how to weave a web.
She tried to weave one
but all she succeeded in making
was a pile of silk.

Zoe had made herself so tired
that she lay down on her pile of silk
and went to sleep.

When Zoe woke up she was very hungry.
"I must try again to make a web," she thought.
"I am so hungry, I must catch a fly."

8

Zoe looked up and saw a bird on a wire.
"That web has caught a very big fly," she thought.
"I will make one like that."

But although she copied it exactly,
the web was not right
and it did not catch any flies.

Then she noticed a cockatoo in a cage. "That looks a good web," she thought. "I will make one like that."

But although she copied it exactly,
the web was not right
and it did not catch any flies.

Looking around, Zoe saw a pig in a little pen.
"What a funny web," she thought.
"But it has caught a very big insect.
I will make one like that."

13

But although she copied it exactly,
the web was not right
and it did not catch any flies.

Along the road, Zoe could see a cow
with its head poking over a gate.
"That is a wonderful web," thought Zoe.
"Look what a big creature it has caught!
I will make one like that."

But although she copied it exactly,
the web was not right
and it did not catch any flies.

Then she spotted a girl lying in a hammock.
"That is a very good web," thought Zoe.
"I will make one like that."

But although she copied it exactly,
the web was not right
and it did not catch any flies.

In the garden behind Zoe,
a large, lace curtain was hanging out to dry.
"Perhaps a web that flaps about will attract flies,"
thought Zoe.
"I will make one like that."

But although she copied it exactly,
the web was not right
and it did not catch any flies.

By this time, Zoe was so disappointed and so hungry that she nearly did not notice a bird swooping down on her.

Just in time, she dodged its sharp beak
and ran to hide under a nearby hedge.

The bird soon flew away
and Zoe cautiously poked her head out
the other side of the hedge.

That was when she noticed
that this side of the hedge
was covered with spider webs.

Zoe had found her family!

Zoe quickly learned how to weave a web —
she copied the other webs exactly!

This web was just right,
and soon Zoe had caught a nice, fat fly.